JUMPING JIVE

"Guaranteed to get you spinning and twirling round your bedroom!"
Alice, 9

"I like the characters very much and am looking forward to the next book."
Eden, 8

"Once you start it, you can't stop reading it!"
Levana, 8

"I enjoyed reading this book because I loved the characters."
Mira, 8

First published in Great Britain in 2012
by Hodder Children's Books

1

A Catalogue record for this book is available from
the British Library

ISBN: 978 1 444 90967 8

Printed and bound by
CPI Group (UK) Ltd, Croydon, CR0 4YY

The paper and board used in this paperback by Hodder Children's
Books are natural recyclable products made from wood grown in
sustainable forests. The manufacturing processes conform to the
environmental regulations of the country of origin.

Hodder Children's Books
a division of Hachette Children's Books
338 Euston Road, London NW1 3BH
An Hachette UK company
www.hachette.co.uk

JUMPING JIVE

Chloe Melody

Hodder
Children's
Books

A division of Hachette Children's Books

★ Meet the Professional Dancers from ★

Robin Windsor

Photo Jon Cottam © BBC 2011

★ **Which three words best describe the jive to you?**

Energetic, ferocious and uplifting.

★ **How old were you when you discovered you loved to dance?**

I was three years old, I started dancing very young!

★ **Did you go to a special dance academy like Bella?**

Yes, I went to the Ipswich School of Dancing which was my local dance school. I spent most of my free time there.

★ **How old were you when you won your first dance competition?**

I was five years old, obviously it wasn't a professional dance competition like the competitions I did as a grown up but it was a fun experience for a little boy and it was wonderful to win.

★ **What is your favourite dance and why?**

The jive because it's a fun, lively dance and I'm a fun, lively person!

Turn the page to find out how Bella learns to dance the jive ...

"Make sure you keep the beat, girls!" Miss Anna clapped her hands in time to the music as the Strictly Dance Academy girls went through their routine for the third time that afternoon. "One and two, three and four," Miss Anna counted out the steps of the complicated samba section in the middle of the dance she'd choreographed for them. Bella took a breath and concentrated as hard as she

could on getting the
steps right. As they
came to the final few
moves of the routine, she
kicked her leg as high as
possible. Miss Anna was
always telling them to "kick
high to the sky!"

Bella raised her arms
for the finishing position
and broke out into an
enormous smile. Every day
at the academy she was
learning something
new and she totally
loved it!

"Excellent dancing
ever*rrr*yone!" Miss

Anna said as the music stopped. "You are working as hard as my students back in Russia!"

Bella grinned over at Sofia and Natalie. She thought how happy she was that she'd met them. Dancing was *always* Bella's favourite thing to do but it was even better when she was dancing right next to her best friends!

Sofia grinned back and Natalie winked – they were enjoying being in the academy every bit as much as Bella.

I really am in the best school in the world, Bella thought. Even after a couple of months, she still found it hard to believe that she really belonged. She remembered when she had come to the auditions with her dad. She had been one of the least experienced girls to try for a place and yet she'd been picked to be in the Strictly Dance Academy! Not only that, but since Bella had started training, she'd been chosen to dance in a carnival with the band New Ride and to perform in a gala performance of a West End musical. Sometimes it felt as if she wasn't so much in a dancing school as on a dancing roller coaster!

Miss Anna clapped her hands again to get their attention. "Now, everyone, make sure you do your stretching exercises properly – we *do not* want any pulled muscles . . ."

Bella shuddered. She couldn't bear the thought of not being able to dance

because of an injury. She was about
to start her stretching routine when
Miss Anna called over. "Bella, Natalie,
Sofia and Veronica, may I see you for a
moment?"

Bella ran over with the other three
girls, her heart thumping. That was the
thing about being in the Strictly Dance
Academy – you never knew what was
going to happen next!

Miss Anna waited for the rest of the
class to leave and then turned to the four
girls. "I have some news for you," she
said, smiling. "A film producer has been
in touch with the academy."

A film producer! Bella felt a buzz of
excitement run through her. *What was
this about?*

"He's looking for some junior dancers for a scene in his new film," Miss Anna went on. "But the problem is, he can't hold regular auditions because the whole project is top secret."

"Top secret?" Sofia asked.

"Yes. Because the star of the film is Jet Rogerson," Miss Anna said.

The four girls gasped. *Jet Rogerson!* Bella's insides did a triple twirl. Jet Rogerson was the most famous actor in the entire world! Not only that, he was also Bella's *favourite* actor in the entire world!

"The film is set during the 1950s and there's a scene set at a prom with a big dance number," Miss Anna continued. "So you'll all learn the routine and then one of you will be chosen to dance it with Jet."

Bella shook her head in shock. She could hardly believe it. She had a poster of Jet Rogerson up on the wall of their dorm and now she was going to get the chance to meet him . . . it was like a dream!

"Whoo-hoo!" Natalie's eyes were shining. "That is a-ma-zing!"

"A chance to be in a Jet Rogerson film?" Sofia said, bouncing on her toes.

"As my mum would say, it's incrrrrrredible!"

Bella laughed. She loved it when Sofia did impressions of her Italian prrrrima ballerina mother!

"It's seriously incredible," Bella said. She felt goosebumps at the back of her neck.

Even Veronica was impressed. "His movies aren't bad at all," she said. "And as I've had quite a bit of acting experience I'm sure being in a film will come naturally for me."

Natalie rolled her eyes and Bella couldn't help smiling. It wasn't the first time Veronica had acted like a diva and it probably wouldn't be the last!

The chance to dance with her

favourite actor in the whole world!
Bella couldn't imagine how life at the
Strictly Dance Academy could get any
more exciting.

2

As the girls waited for Miss Anna to explain what would happen next, Bella kept picturing Jet Rogerson as he looked on her poster – with his dark blue eyes and his shock of jet-black hair. Was it really possible she was going to meet him in person? She had to force herself to stop daydreaming and listen to Miss Anna.

"I talked it over with the school principal, Mr Goodwin," Miss Anna told them. "We felt that the four of you are not only talented enough to be considered, but you have all been working extremely hard. That's why we chose you for these secret tryouts."

Bella shivered with excitement. Mr Ben Goodwin thought she was good enough to audition for a movie starring Jet Rogerson! This really was her best day at the academy yet!

"Now," Miss Anna went on briskly. "There's no time to lose. Your first day on set is this afternoon. You'll be meeting the set choreographer and learning the dance today, and then tomorrow you'll have the audition."

"Tomorrow?" Bella felt her heart race. There was so little time to get ready!

Miss Anna smiled. "Don't worry, you'll all be fine."

"What kind of dance will we be doing?" Bella asked.

"A really fun one!" Miss Anna said. "The jive!"

"Ooh, that's one of my all-time favourites!" called a familiar voice.

Bella looked up to see Pam, the cleaning lady at the Strictly Dance Academy. She walked up with a pair of dusters in her hand.

"You'll have to be quick on your feet for the jive," Pam warned them, shaking a duster at Bella.

"That's true," Miss Anna agreed. "It's a very quick dance, and needs excellent foot work."

"Of course, if you have dainty feet like mine, you'll be fine," Pam sing-songed, chuckling. She held out one of her feet for inspection. "No matter how quick they flick, don't forget to point!"

"We won't," Bella promised.

Pam's wrinkled face broke into a wide smile. "I'm sure you'll all do very well. In fact, you'll be *a-mazing*!"

The girls and Miss Anna laughed as Pam waved goodbye with her dusters. At the door she did a little kick and then disappeared.

"Right, girls, you need to get going if you're going to be amazing!" Miss Anna said.

Bella grinned. She couldn't wait to get started!

*

That afternoon, on the bus to the set, Bella
looked up the jive on her smartphone.
Even though she had been working hard
at her dancing ever since starting at the
Strictly Academy, Bella still felt totally
behind the other girls. They had all had
proper dance training before the academy
auditions while Bella had only done a few
after-school clubs. There was still so much
she didn't know – including the jive! So
Bella wanted to try and be as prepared as
possible before they met the set
choreographer.

   *Though even if I knew the dance really
well I'd still be nervous*, Bella thought.
Thinking about seeing Jet Rogerson
set her heart racing again. She double

checked that she was wearing her lucky,
sparkly heart-shaped earrings. She was
definitely going to need their luck today!
To calm herself down, Bella tried to
focus on the page of facts about the jive.
But Sofia, Natalie and Veronica were so
excited that she found it hard to
concentrate.

"I can't wait, I can't
wait, I can't wait!"
Sofia chanted. "A real
studio! A real film!"

"I know!"
Natalie said. "I
can't *believe* we
can't tell anyone
– if I could text
my friends in

America they'd go crazy!"

Veronica got out some make-up from her bag and started to put it on. "You should really do the same, you know," she told them. "You don't want to look like a complete amateur in front of an international star – even if that's what you are," she added, glancing at Bella.

Veronica held some bright red lipstick to her lips but as the bus turned a corner her hand jerked, making the lipstick smudge across her cheek.

"Maybe it's better to look like an amateur than to look like a clown," Natalie drawled.

Sofia laughed and Bella gave Natalie a grateful smile. Veronica had been making mean comments about her since they all started at the academy but Natalie and Sofia always defended her – Bella felt so lucky to have such loyal friends.

"Remember that song Jet sang in *Friday Nights*?" Sofia said, leaning against the window and smiling dreamily. "The one in the diner?"

"You mean the one that went like this?" Natalie started humming.

"Yes!" Sofia started singing along with her and even Veronica joined in. They sang at the top of their voices.

When they were finished, Bella laughed. "Great singing but can you help me learn a bit about the jive before we get there? I still don't know enough about it."

"OK, OK," Natalie said. "The main thing you need to know is that the jive is *fast*."

"Super fast," Sofia agreed. "It's the fastest of all the Latin dances."

"I just hope you'll be able to keep up," Veronica said. "It's *very* demanding."

"You'll be *fine*," Natalie said firmly, shooting a look at Veronica. "Basically it's just lots of knee-lifts, bends, kicks and flicks."

"The webpage said it has a six-beat pattern with eight weight changes," Bella said. "It sounds really complicated."

"It just makes it easy to fall over!" Natalie laughed.

"It's good fun," Sofia said. "You'll love it. But we're definitely going to need all the energy we can get."

Bella took a breath to ask more when Natalie suddenly squealed. "Look! I think we're there!"

"Finally," Veronica said.

Bella pressed her nose to the window as the bus turned into a narrow road leading up to a large concrete building. A sign by the entrance said "Welcome to Salcombe School" in dark blue letters. Next to the building was a large playground.

"This isn't a studio," Veronica said. "It's a school."

"But that's even better!" Natalie said, grinning. "That means we're on *location!*"

"Yes," Miss Anna came up the aisle to where they were sitting. "That's why it's all top secret. If anyone found out there's a film shoot here with Jet then the whole school would be mobbed with fans and the press. And of course that would make it impossible to get any work done."

"I can just imagine all the fans lining up to get his autograph," said Sofia.

Yes, and if I wasn't here to audition, I'd probably be one of them, thought Bella, smiling.

3

As the bus pulled in through the gates of the school and drew up in the car park, Bella felt her stomach twist with nerves. Suddenly she felt overwhelmed. The closer they got to the film set, the more Bella wondered if she should be there at all. There was no way she was good enough to be dancing in a Jet Rogerson film. And what would she say to him when she met him?

Luckily, Bella didn't have time to think about it too much. Miss Anna hurried the four of them off the bus and through the main entrance to the school. A man dressed in black jeans and a black polo-neck greeted them as they came in, ticking their names off a list on the clipboard he was holding. He waved them along the corridor. "Just keep on going until you get to the gym – you can't miss it," he told them.

Bella saw what he meant as they drew closer. The doors to the gym were wide open and there were people hurrying in and out, carrying all kinds of equipment – cameras, lights, heaps of material and costumes. Everyone looked busy and efficient and again Bella couldn't help wondering if she really belonged there. As Miss Anna led them through the doors the girls gasped.

The walls of the gym were hung with swathes of deep purple and silver cloth, and fastened by bunches of silver flowers. Above their heads the whole ceiling had been covered with a dark blue velvet cloth studded with crystal stars. Little round tables with pale lavender cloths dotted the edges of the gym with chairs upholstered in the same material.

"This is the set for the scene at the school dance," Miss Anna told them.

"Wow!" Natalie whistled. "It's fabulous!"

"Totally fabulous!" Bella said, forgetting her nerves for a moment as she took the scene in. She could just imagine coming to a school dance here, in an amazing dress, and then dancing all night . . . it would be the best dream ever!

Just then, Bella caught sight of a boy with dark hair coming in from a door at the other end of the gym. It was Jet!

Bella felt as if her heart had stopped beating for a second as he came closer. Her skin grew hot. *I can't believe it's really him!* she thought. As he walked towards them he broke into a wide smile and held out his hand. "Hi there, I'm Jet. You must be the dancers who have come to my rescue!"

Miss Anna introduced the four girls and Jet shook hands with them all. Bella felt as if her face was on fire as he shook her hand. And her legs went so wobbly they were like jelly! Worst of all, she couldn't think of a thing to say when he smiled and said, "Nice to meet you."

"I'm a really big fan of all your work," Veronica told Jet, tossing back her blonde hair.

"Well, thanks, that's really nice of you," Jet smiled. "I'm always nervous that the next film's going to be a complete flop though!"

"That's not possible," Sofia said.

 *"Everyone* loves your movies." "Totally loves them!" Natalie agreed.

Bella wished she could think of
something to say but her mind was a
complete blank. She felt totally tongue-
tied!

"Do you have a favourite co-star,
or are you still looking for the perfect
one?" Veronica asked, twirling one of
her blonde curls around her fingers.
Natalie shook her head and grinned.
"Unbelievable!" she whispered to Bella.

Even though Bella was feeling dazed
by the film star's presence, she had to
suppress a giggle. Veronica was really
going all out to try and charm Jet.

"I've really enjoyed working with
everyone on all the films I've made," Jet
said easily. "It's always great to get the
chance to meet new people – like you

guys!" He gave them all a big smile.

He's not only gorgeous, he's really nice! Bella thought. Whoever did end up dancing with him would be super lucky.

A tall woman with a mass of bright red hair dressed in dancing leggings and a loose grey top strode up to them. "Hi – I'm Sasha. Are you the dancers from the Strictly Dance Academy?"

"Yes, that's right," Miss Anna told her. "These are our best and hardest working girls so we hope you'll find them suitable."

"I'm sure we will," said Sasha. "We like hard workers here." She gestured for them to follow her to the middle of the gym while Miss Anna waved goodbye and went off to talk to the director.

Bella noticed that Sasha was carrying a small CD player, which she set on the floor. *We're going to be practising in front of everyone!* Bella realised. Her legs suddenly turned to jelly again – she just hoped they'd stand up to learning such an energetic dance!

"The most important thing is to listen to the rhythm of the music," Sasha told them. "The basic jive has a six-beat pattern – a rock step, which counts as '1, 2' and then two triple steps, '3 and 4' and '5 and 6'. But the best thing is for you to see that in action first."

Sasha turned to Jet. "Jet, you know the dance pretty well now, don't you? Will you help me demonstrate?"

"Sure," Jet grinned. "Don't laugh at me too hard," he told the girls as they prepared to watch.

Sasha pressed play on the machine. As the music started, she and Jet began to dance. The routine seemed to have hundreds of tiny steps and Sasha and Jet didn't stop twisting and turning from start to finish! Their legs flicked out sharply in sets of kicks and flicks and Bella suddenly understood what everyone had meant by the jive being an energetic dance – she felt out of breath just watching!

Bella was mesmerised. She couldn't believe what a good dancer Jet was. He looked like he'd been doing it for years!

At the end of the routine, Sasha stopped the music and turned to the four girls. "What do you think?"

"It's fantastic!" Sofia said, her

eyes shining with excitement.

Natalie and Veronica also looked unfazed and enthusiastic.

It's only me who doesn't know if I can do it, Bella thought miserably.

"Well, let's get on!" Sasha said. She quickly took the four girls through the routine, breaking it down into sections. Bella tried her hardest to concentrate but she was feeling so jittery that she kept forgetting what came next.

After going through it a few times, Sasha stopped. "Right, I think you've got the idea, let's see each of you do a little of the routine on your own."

"Right away?" Bella was horrified. She didn't think she'd learned the routine properly at all!

✳ ✳ ✳ 32 ✳ ✳ ✳

"Don't worry, I don't expect you to have picked up every single part of the routine – not yet anyway!" said Sasha. "Just do the first few steps so I can see how you might shape up. I have very high expectations for the four of you but I'm sure you can live up to them."

"Honestly, if I can do it, anyone can," Jet said. He gave Bella an encouraging smile.

Bella tried to smile back but she could hardly meet his eyes. She felt so shy and awkward in front of him. She couldn't seem to forget that this was Jet Rogerson, famous film star. Even her hands had started to tremble. She didn't think she'd ever been so nervous – not even for the Strictly Dance Academy auditions!

Veronica went first, and managed the first part of the routine well. Natalie and Sofia followed, and seemed to remember the steps without any problems too. Bella's spirits were sinking by the second – she really didn't think she could remember anything.

"Now, Bella, let's see what you can do," Sasha said, beckoning her forwards.

Bella stepped towards Sasha and almost stumbled. Her feet felt like they'd doubled in size!

She heard Veronica giggle behind her. Natalie whispered, "Don't worry, Bella, you'll be fine!"

Sasha clicked on the CD player and Bella began to dance the steps she'd seen the others do. But her legs seemed to be made of cotton wool – instead of flicking out in sharp, high kicks, her feet were hardly lifting off the floor. After a few moments, Bella stopped and shook her head. "I'm sorry," she said. "I just can't remember anything right now."

"Never mind," Sasha said briskly. "Let's take a break for a few minutes. It's a lot to take in all at once." She came forward and patted Bella on the shoulder. "Not to worry, sometimes it takes a while to pick it up."

Bella nodded, feeling her cheeks burn. Sasha was just being kind – Bella knew her dancing had been a complete disaster. Jet must think she was the worst dancer in the whole world!

4

Bella slowly followed Natalie, Sofia
and Veronica to the refreshment station
which had been set up near the doors to
the gym. She was so embarrassed by her
bad dancing that she could hardly take
her eyes off the floor.

"Well, that went well, for *some* of us,"
Veronica announced, reaching for a
bottle of water. "I'm glad *I* didn't look
like an amateur." She gave Bella a

sneering look and Bella felt her cheeks flame up again.

But she's right, Bella thought. *I did look like an amateur.*

Natalie put a hand on Bella's arm, "Don't pay any attention to Veronica. She's just jealous because Jet hasn't been making a big fat fuss over her. You'll be fine after you've had a break."

"You won't just be fine – you'll be ma*rrr*vellous!" Sofia said in her best mock Italian accent.

Bella gave them both a wobbly smile. She knew her friends were trying to make her feel better but she didn't feel so sure that she would be any better after the break. Dancing in front of a mega movie star was turning out to be seriously terrifying!

Jet, who had been talking with Sasha, now walked up to them.

"Hey, do you have a minute?" he said softly to Bella. "I was hoping we could have a quick chat."

"Um, OK," Bella said.

He's going to tell me that I'm not good enough to rehearse with the others and that I should go back to the academy, she thought.

Her eyes stung with tears as she followed Jet to a couple of chairs in the corner of the gym. "I'm really sorry about the rehearsal," Bella blurted out as soon as they had sat down. "I know I made a complete mess of it."

To Bella's surprise, Jet laughed. "You

think that was a mess?" He shook his head. "You should have seen me on my first ever movie – now *that* was a mess!" He grinned. "I was so nervous I couldn't remember a single one of my lines, not one word. It was *seriously* embarrassing. All those people watching me and I was just standing there, opening and

shutting my mouth like a goldfish!"

Jet pulled such a funny face that Bella couldn't help giggling.

"What happened?" she asked.

"I took a break. Called my mom. She told me to remember that I loved acting – to forget that there was anyone else in the room and just be the person I was supposed to be."

"Oh!" Bella exclaimed. "That's just like what my dad told me when I was auditioning for the academy – to dance like nobody's watching!"

"Exactly!" Jet said. "So keep going because you'll definitely get there in the end. Just remember, if I can do those kicks and flicks, a really talented dancer like you can."

A really talented dancer!

Bella's cheeks were red again but this time it wasn't because she felt ashamed, it was because she felt proud!

"Thanks, Jet," Bella said.

"Hey, it's no problem. We professionals have got to support each other, right?" Jet grinned and Bella beamed back. As they walked back to the others, Bella realised she didn't feel shy of Jet anymore. Now that she wasn't so overwhelmed, she knew she could dance again. Besides, if Jet thought she was a professional, then Bella was determined to act like one.

"Right, then," Sasha said. "Let's go through the routine a few more times."

Just before they started, Bella closed

her eyes for a second. She pretended
that no one else was in the room. She
took a deep breath and realised
that her legs didn't feel
like jelly but strong and
straight. As the music
began, Bella found
herself remembering
the routine more and more.
She even remembered to
keep her toes pointed in
the kicks just like Pam had
told her!

By the last run
through, Bella was
dancing with an
enormous smile on her
face. Jet looked over at her

and gave her a thumbs-up sign and she beamed back at him.

No matter what happens now, at least I know I've tried my hardest, thought Bella. She was so glad she'd kept on trying even though she hadn't felt sure she could do it.

"Well done all of you, you've really got it," Sasha said. She nodded approvingly at them. "I think you can all take another break for a few minutes – grab yourself some water." As Sasha passed Bella she smiled. "Well done, Bella, that was great."

"Thank you!" Bella went into the break feeling much more like her normal enthusiastic self. Maybe dancing on a film set really was like dancing anywhere else. You just had to learn it well, and then relax and enjoy it! Bella took some water and then, seeing Sofia didn't have any, picked up another bottle to offer to her. As Bella walked up with it, she saw that Sofia had her phone cradled in her hand and was texting.

"Hey, Sofia!" Bella said. She held out the bottle of water. "I thought you might need this."

Sofia jumped. "Oh! You gave me a shock!" Sofia quickly stuffed her phone back into her pocket.

"Thanks for the water though."

"No problem," Bella told her. She couldn't help thinking her friend looked guilty as she fidgeted with the pocket where she'd put her phone.

I wonder who she's been texting? Bella remembered how Natalie had talked about wanting to tell all her friends in America. Did that give Sofia the idea of telling someone? Bella really hoped Sofia hadn't been breaking the rules and texting about the film with Jet . . .

But before Bella could ask Sofia any questions, Miss Anna approached them. "Right girls, I've been talking to the director. It looks like there's time for one more session to rehearse the dance this afternoon and then tomorrow we'll come back to do the actual filming."

Bella stopped thinking about her suspicions about Sofia. The idea of filming made her feel as if she had a billion butterflies in her stomach. Tomorrow she'd have to prove herself – it really would be time for action!

Back at the academy, Bella snuck into an empty rehearsal room to try and practise her steps. She was determined to prepare as much as she could for the next day. Jet had told her he believed in her – she couldn't let him down!

Bella was just starting to go through the routine when someone coughed behind her. She spun round, startled, and then smiled when she saw Jason at the door.

"Sorry to interrupt – I just had to find out how it all went. It's not every day your dance partner goes off to jive with a film star!" Jason said as he came in. "We've been feeling jealous of the four of you all day!" He smiled. "But I bet you really impressed them all."

Bella shook her head, her stomach sinking as she thought of her first attempt to do the dance. "To be honest, it was a bit of a disaster at the beginning," she told him, her cheeks turning hot at the memory.

"Why? What happened?"

Bella found herself spilling out every moment of the day – her attack of shyness, her nervousness, and the terrible rehearsal when her legs just wouldn't do what they were told.

Jason listened sympathetically. "Well you were fine in the end, and Jet sounds like a really nice guy," he said when Bella had finished. "And I know you'll be brilliant at the audition." He grinned at her. "But how about we make sure of that by practising the dance now? I've done the jive quite a lot so I think I'll be able to keep up!"

Bella's spirits lifted – telling Jason about the day had brought her nerves right back but if she could go through the routine with her favourite partner she just knew she'd feel better.

"That would be great!"

"Right then," Jason said. "Show me how it goes."

Taking Jason through the dance proved to Bella that she knew the routine more thoroughly than she'd realised. Slowly, she started to relax and enjoy herself, and by the end of their rehearsal together, Bella was grinning.

"That was fantastic!" Jason told her as they finished. "You're definitely ready to be filmed with a superstar!"

"Thanks for helping me out," Bella told him. "I feel *much* better about the dance now."

"No problem," Jason said. "You just have to promise to help me if I ever get to dance with Britney Sparkle! If I got to dance with someone famous that's who I'd pick . . ."

Bella laughed. "I don't think you'd need any help!"

She left the rehearsal room beaming. With Jet's confidence in her, and Jason's help practising, maybe tomorrow she *could* dance like a real professional . . .

*

The next morning, the four girls were on the bus on their way to the set by 6 a.m.

"That's what I hate about working on films, you have to get up *so* early," Veronica said with a big yawn.

"Right, because you work on films all the time," Natalie said with an extravagant eye roll that made Bella and Sofia giggle.

Veronica tossed her hair and started going through her bag, taking out bits of make-up.

"Remember that there will be make-up and costume artists there to make you look the part today," Miss Anna said, leaning over from her seat.

"Oh, of course!" Veronica looked delighted at the thought of being made up by a real film make-up artist.

Bella was buzzing with nerves. *But at least this time I'm not feeling terrified*, she thought. Her talk with Jet and her practice session with Jason had helped her get past her wobbles yesterday. Now she decided to concentrate on why she was at the academy in the first place – because she adored dancing!

At the school, the girls were ushered off the bus and straight through to the costume area which had been set up in an empty classroom. Miss Anna told them she would meet them at the end of the day and wished them good luck before going off to talk to some of the production team.

Clothing rails filled the room, each one hung with a variety of clothes in every kind of style and colour. Bella spotted a rack with shirts and trousers, all pinned with labels – "Jet Rogerson: Scene 2, Jet Rogerson: Scene 15". She shivered with excitement – somehow seeing those labels made the film seem real, instead of just a dream.

Sasha was there to greet them, looking very professional in a pair of black trousers and a fitted red blouse. She was with a young woman dressed in a purple jersey skirt and a sweater with a large yellow heart on it.

"Good morning!" Sasha said. "This is Naomi, our costume designer. She'll be making sure you have the right costumes for the prom scene."

"It's really nice to meet you," Naomi

told them with a bright smile. "I'm really looking forward to helping you get ready!"

Bella thought Naomi looked super cool in her outfit – she was just glad that she seemed super friendly as well!

"Right, let's go and pick out your outfits for the dance," Naomi said. She led them to the back of the room. A rack of costumes hung on a rail with a sign on the first hanger that read "Scene 20: Prom".

When Bella saw the sign, she couldn't help wondering which one of them would be dancing with Jet. How would it feel to dance in front of all the lights and cameras next to him?

Naomi beckoned them forward and got the girls to stand in a row while she held up the prom dresses against them. "All these dresses are modelled on a 1950s style that's perfect for this dance," she told them. "They have lots of netting underneath so that they stick out."

Bella loved the pretty corsages that sat
at the waist of the dresses and the way
the skirt part went out underneath. They
were just right for showing off all the
quick kicks and flicks in the dance.

"Hmm, I think with your lovely blonde
hair, you'll really suit this turquoise

blue," Naomi told Veronica. Veronica was delighted and took the outfit off to the changing area to try on.

Naomi picked an emerald green dress for Sofia and a burnt orange dress for Natalie. For Bella, she chose a deep pink dress with a sequined waist band above a skirt covered in layers of pretty frills. The girls quickly changed and ten minutes later stood in front of an approving Naomi. Bella stared at their reflection in the mirror – they really did look like girls going to a school dance now!

"Wonderful – now for the final touches!" Naomi said.

She led them to another room where the girls had towels wrapped around their neck and shoulders while their

hair and make-up was done in front of
mirrors framed with bulbs.

"It's like a real star's dressing room!"
Bella said.

"I could really get used to this!"
Natalie drawled, leaning back in her
chair.

Bella couldn't help noticing
that Sofia was still texting
on her phone while she
was waiting for her turn
to be made up. She really
hoped she wasn't
texting anything
about the filming.
The last thing
she wanted
was to see

Sofia get into trouble . . .

As soon as the girls were ready, Naomi took them back to the gym where Sasha was waiting for them.

"Right, let's see the routine from the top," she told them.

This time, Bella found it much easier to forget that they were surrounded by people with cameras and clipboards. When the music started, Bella pretended she was a girl dancing at her school's prom and having the most wonderful time. At the end of the dance, Bella realised that she had remembered every single step!

"Wow!"

Bella turned to see Jet in his prom suit costume. He bowed and gave

them a round of applause.
"You look
fantastic!" he
told them.
"Yes, and they all
danced fabulously," Sasha
said. "So now I just have
to tell you who you will be
dancing with, Jet."
Bella felt her breath
catch in her throat. She
couldn't help hoping
that she might have a chance, even
though she'd got off to such a bad start.
But did Sasha think she had improved
enough?

Before Sasha could speak, a loud
banging noise made all of them jump.

"What was that?" Sasha said, hurrying over to the window. "The location manager is supposed to be making sure there's no noise during the filming."

Bella, Natalie, Sofia and Veronica followed Sasha to the window with Jet close behind.

"Jet! Jet!" The sound of screaming started up outside.

"Uh-oh," Jet took a step back from the window. "It looks like the fans have found me."

Sasha frowned. "This is the last thing we need – this location was supposed to be kept top secret!"

A young woman wearing jeans and a sweatshirt that had "production assistant" on it in red letters came

running across the gym. "They've gotten
inside the school!"

"Jet, you and the girls better find
somewhere to hide until we manage to
clear the school," Sasha said briskly.

"Let's get going," Jet said. He set
off at a run to the door, with the four
girls close behind. In the hallway, Jet
stopped and looked round. "I'm really
sorry about this," he told them. "You
weren't supposed to spend your day here
running away from fans!"

Bella shook her head. She knew it
wasn't his fault that the news had got
out about the filming. *I just hope it
wasn't because of Sofia*, she thought.

There was another loud bang.

The main entrance doors had been

pushed open. Streaming into the
school was a crowd of what looked like
hundreds of girls, all screaming
Jet's name!

6

The girls spotted Jet immediately and
started running down the hall. Bella
found herself pushed back against the
wall as a group of girls surrounded Jet.
Jet raised his hands to try and calm
them down but they shrieked even
louder. Bella couldn't see Natalie, Sofia
or Veronica so she took a breath and
plunged into the crowd. She wove her
way through the tightly packed girls

until she was close enough to grab Jet's sleeve.

"Up there!" she shouted, pointing up at the staircase behind him.

He nodded. They pushed their way through the circle of fans and started up the staircase, taking them three at a time. At the top of the steps she paused for a moment to take another breath.

"Crazy, huh?" Jet whispered in her ear. "Welcome to my world!"

Bella looked down at the fans who were frantically trying to follow them but held back because there were so many of them crowded together. "Totally crazy!" Bella couldn't help giggling. The mob of girls were jumping up and down and pulling at their hair, still screaming at the top of their voices. It was all so silly!

A few of the girls managed to push their way on to the stairs and started to make their way up.

"We'd better keep going," Jet said.

He and Bella started to run again. They dashed through three empty classrooms and then down another long hallway. At the end of the hall was a heavy steel door. Jet managed to pull it open and peered outside. "There's another staircase here."

"Let's try it," Bella said.

The staircase took them to the back door of the gym. The production assistant who'd told them about the fans was standing there, watching out for them. "Oh great, you're back!" she said, looking relieved. "We've managed to get all the fans gathered in the other hallway – we're just trying to get them to keep quiet now so filming can start."

"Great," Jet said. He turned to Bella. "Hey, thanks for your help back there – I wouldn't have escaped without you!"

"That's OK," Bella told him, starting to laugh. She had never imagined that meeting Jet Rogerson would end up with her on the run from a bunch of screaming fans!

They went into the gym together and Bella saw Natalie, Sofia and Veronica waiting with Sasha. Veronica scowled when she saw Bella walk in with Jet but Natalie and Sofia just grinned. "Glad you made it back in one piece!" Natalie said. "Those fans are pretty scary!"

"Yes, I'm glad you made it back too," Sasha told Bella. "Especially as I'd like you to partner Jet in the dance."

"You would?" Bella could hardly believe it.

"Yes," Sasha said, smiling. "I really would."

Bella beamed. "Thank you so much!"

She felt almost dizzy for a second. It really was a dream come true!

"You don't have to thank me," Sasha said. "It's all down to you working so hard to get it right."

Sasha went off to talk to the director and Natalie and Sofia immediately grabbed Bella's hands and whirled her round.

"Well done! That's fantastic!" Sofia said.

"Do you promise to still be friends with us when you're famous?" teased Natalie.

"Well done," Veronica muttered, but she was scowling as she turned away.

"Don't worry about the grumpy diva," Natalie said. "She's just green with envy!"

The production assistant rushed up to them. "It's time to take your places. The director wants to try and get this scene done quickly in case there are any more disturbances."

The four girls ran to the centre of the gym, where Jet was waiting with the three boys who were to dance with Natalie, Sofia and Veronica.

"Let's try and get this scene done in a couple of takes, everyone," the director shouted. He strode up to Bella. "Hi, Bella. Sasha tells me you know the routine thoroughly so we're going to try and get it taped before those fans get in the way." He shook his head. "If I find out who leaked our location . . ." he muttered, as he walked over to the camera man.

Bella gulped. She glanced back at Sofia and hoped more than ever that she hadn't been the one who told the fans where Jet was.

There was no more time to worry about Sofia because the director was motioning them all to take their places. Bella felt relaxed and happy inside. She

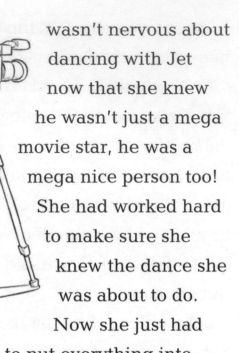

wasn't nervous about dancing with Jet now that she knew he wasn't just a mega movie star, he was a mega nice person too! She had worked hard to make sure she knew the dance she was about to do. Now she just had to put everything into making sure she did it as well as she possibly could. Bella felt as if she was floating on a balloon of happiness . . .

Sasha cued the music and the director called "Action!" Immediately the fans started screaming outside the door. It was as if they thought the director had been directing them!

The director groaned. "This cannot be happening."

The production team ran to the door to try and convince the fans to be quiet. They waved from the door as soon as the shouting had died down and the director clapped his hands. "OK, let's give this another try . . . and *action*!"

This time the music started and they were able to dance

the first three bars of the song before
the screaming started again.

"Jet! Jet! Jet!"

"CUT!" the director shouted. His
face was flushed and he looked furious
as he stalked up to where Bella and
Jet stood. "This is *impossible!*" He
slapped his hand against his thigh.
"We're not going to get anything done
if those fans keep interrupting. We
might just have to cut this scene
altogether."

Cut the scene! If the director cut
the scene then Bella's chance of
dancing with Jet was gone for ever.
She knew she'd never get an
opportunity like this again. Bella's
floating feeling of happiness had

completely deflated. She blinked back tears as the director walked away, muttering under his breath. It looked like Bella's new role was gone for good!

7

Jet came up to Bella and put his hand on her shoulder. "Hey, are you OK?"

Bella gave him a watery smile. "I'm all right. Just a bit disappointed that the scene is going to be cut. I was really looking forward to it."

"Me too," Jet told her. "Look, don't give up yet. I've got an idea. Just stick with me." He turned round to Natalie, Sofia and Veronica. "Do you guys want

to come with me? I'm going to try and fix this." *What is he planning to do?* Bella wondered. She had no idea how Jet was going to manage to get a huge crowd of fanatic fans to disappear. Bella crossed her fingers and made a silent wish that whatever Jet's idea was, it would work!

The four girls followed Jet as he ran to the doors at the end of the gym and whispered something to the production assistant standing guard against the hoard of fans. The production assistant frowned but as Jet kept talking she smiled and nodded. Then she opened the doors and Jet stepped right into the crowd!

Bella, Natalie, Sofia and Veronica kept close behind as Jet walked forward. There was a surge of screams as the fans realised what had happened.

"I hope he knows what he's doing," Natalie whispered to Bella.

So do I! Bella thought.

But then Jet held up his hands and amazingly the shouting died down.

"OK," he said loudly. "I'm going to sign some autographs for a few minutes, OK? But please, try and stay calm!"

The crowd of girls began to thrust notebooks and pads and scraps of paper at Jet as he took a pen out of his pocket. As he started to sign his name again and again, he chatted with some of the girls nearest to him, asking them if they liked music and telling them the names of his favourite bands.

Bella listened, thinking again that Jet might be a superstar but was a super kind person too!

As Bella stood next to him, a girl reached out and pulled her sleeve. "Excuse me, will you sign my notebook?"

Bella couldn't believe it – just standing next to Jet had made the fans think she must be famous as well!

After Jet had signed his name for what seemed like the millionth time he waved at the crowd to get their attention. "Do you know what would be fun?" Jet called out. "Why don't we sing my favourite song from *Friday Nights*?" He started to sing the same song Sofia, Natalie and Veronica had sung on the bus the day before.

"Did you hear that?" Sofia said to Bella. "It's his favourite song!"

This time, Bella sang along too. As the crowd of fans swayed in time with the song, Bella couldn't help grinning. This was exactly like a scene in a movie!

When the song was finished, Jet

grabbed a chair leaning next to the wall and jumped up on it. "Listen everyone," he said. "It's so great that you came to visit me on set and I want to thank you all for your support," he paused and looked around at the fans with a serious look on his face. "But this movie won't get made unless I go back to work. And the thing is, it has to be completely quiet outside when we film. So I hope you'll understand if I ask you to go home now – so that we can make sure there's another movie for you to come and see me in!"

As Jet finished speaking, the fans gave a deafening cheer. Then as Jet called goodbye, the crowd began to file slowly out of the school, chattering excitedly to each other as they went.

Jet jumped back off the chair. He grinned at Bella. "There, I think that's that problem taken care of. Now, I think *you* owe me a dance!"

Bella just hoped the director would still want to see it!

The four girls followed Jet back into the gym where the director was pacing up and down in front of the cameras. "The fans are going now, so we're all set to do the scene," Jet told him.

The director narrowed his eyes suspiciously. "They're really going?"

Sasha came up to them. "Whatever Jet said to them has worked, the production team say the fans will be off the premises in five minutes!"

The director straightened up. "Well, if that's really the case then let's give the scene a go." He looked at Bella and started to smile. "Be a shame to waste those nice costumes wouldn't it? And besides, Sasha's been telling me how hard you girls have been practising this dance so I'd like to see it!"

"Thank you!" Bella said, breaking into a wide smile.

"OK, just be ready to go when I call 'action'!" he said.

Bella nodded and ran to take her position again. Inside, she felt the familiar rush of excitement she always felt just before a performance. But this time it was extra special. She was about to dance in one of the biggest movies of the year with the world's biggest movie star. Bella thought this might just be the most exciting day of her life!

8

This time when the director called
"Action!" everything went perfectly.
Bella felt her legs flicking out sharply
in time to the music as she and

Jet twisted and turned.
Jet grinned at her
and it made Bella's
smile even bigger.
It really did feel as

if Bella was at the most amazing school dance – and she was the belle of the ball! As she started the last set of kicks, Bella put every bit of energy she had into them – she wanted the dance to look as much fun as it felt!

The music came to the end and the director called "Cut!"

Jet stepped forward and pulled Bella into a huge hug.

"That was fantastic," he whispered. "I told you you'd get there in the end!"

Bella felt she might

burst with happiness as she hugged him back.

"That was great!" The director rushed up to them both. "Thank goodness you managed to deal with the fans, Jet,

because it would be a crime not to include this scene in the film. It's perfect!"

Bella thought she must be positively glowing as the director told them they'd have a quick break and then do another take of the scene.

Bella walked with the others to the refreshment station to get some water. There had been so much going on that she was definitely in need of a drink! As she sipped from her bottle of water she noticed Sofia pulling out her phone again and beginning to text. Bella moved closer but Sofia turned away, craning over her phone as if trying to keep what she was doing a secret.

Oh no! Bella thought. *I must stop her!*

"Sofia!" Bella whispered. "Please don't

text any more. If the fans come back again the director will definitely stop filming."

"What?" Sofia turned round with a puzzled frown. "But why would the fans come back?"

Bella faltered. "You're not telling people about the filming?"

Sofia shook her head. "No, of course not! I've been texting my brother because we're trying to decide what to get my mum for her birthday!"

Bella felt her cheeks go red. "Oh, I'm so sorry, Sofia, it's just that I kept seeing you texting as if you were hiding from people . . ."

Sofia laughed. "That was just because I thought I'd get into trouble with Sasha for not keeping focussed on the dancing.

You know how strict Miss Anna is about texting at the academy. But Mum's birthday is really soon so I needed to get her present sorted out. That's why I've been texting so much."

"Oh, I see," Bella said. She felt terrible for not trusting her friend. "I'm really sorry – I should have known you wouldn't tell anyone."

"Don't worry," Sofia said. "After all, somebody obvious *did* text – why else would all those fans turn up?"

"I wonder who it was," Bella mused. "I wouldn't have thought anyone working on the film would do it – they could get into so much trouble."

Just then, there was a loud clattering behind them. Bella and Sofia turned to see Veronica straightening up after banging into a piece of the set. In her hand was her phone and she was holding it up and pointing it right at – Jet!

"Trying to take a picture of Jet," Sofia said softly. "Hmm, I wonder what else Veronica's been up to . . ."

Bella giggled. "I think the mystery is solved!"

The director clapped his hands. "All

right, everyone, time for the next take. Let's make it as fabulous as the last one!"

Bella grinned at Sofia as they ran to take their beginning positions. It didn't matter who had told the fans about the filming. All that mattered now was that Bella was about to get back to her dream come true – dancing with the superstar Jet!

*

When Miss Anna took them to a private screening of the film a few months later, Bella thought she might burst with excitement – she could hardly believe they were going to see themselves on the big screen!

"I hope I got some decent close-ups," Veronica said, as the four girls sank down into the velvet seats with their boxes of popcorn and bottles of water.

I just hope I got the steps right! thought Bella. Her stomach lurched as the lights in the cinema dimmed and the credits started to roll across the screen.

Natalie nudged Bella. "Can you believe you're about to see yourself dancing with Jet up there?"

"No!" Bella whispered. Her heart was beating so fast it felt like it was doing the jive all by itself!

The girls fell silent as the film began and Bella wondered if the others were feeling as nervous as she was. But soon she was so lost in the story that when the dance scene came on she was startled – was that girl up there with Jet really her? She held her breath as she watched herself twirl and kick at top speed across the screen with Jet matching every move beside her.

As the scene came to an end, Miss Anna leaned over to whisper to the four girls. "Pam was right, you were *a-mazing*!"

Bella beamed to herself in the dark. All the hard work had really paid off in the end – for once she was sure she hadn't put a foot wrong!

See how Bella and her friends
learn to salsa in

Read on for a sneak peek ...

"Let me hear you say HEY!
   I wanna dance the night away.
   HEY! And we can dance all through
   the day . . ."
It was early Friday morning and Bella
Jones and her three roommates, Sofia,
Natalie and Veronica, were singing
at the tops of their voices as they got
dressed for school. The day before,
Veronica's parents had sent her a

brand new MP3 player and she'd been downloading all her favourite tunes. This was the latest Britney Sparkle song 'Dance the Night Away', with the catchiest chorus Bella had ever heard. You couldn't help but dance to it!

"HEY!" Veronica sang into her hairbrush, wiggling her bottom. "I wanna dance the night away."

Bella smiled. She and Veronica had clashed when they'd first met, back at the auditions for the Strictly Dance Academy.

Veronica had given Bella a hard time for not having had years of dance training. Lately, though, she'd been a lot nicer, especially when she loosened up and didn't take herself so seriously. Judging by the shimmies and wiggles currently on display, now was definitely one of those times!

The four girls were students at the academy and loved living there – it was always so fun and exciting! Bella had been worried she might miss her family and friends back home but as it turned out, she was always so busy with her studies and dance lessons that she barely had time to miss a thing. She wouldn't change places for the world.

Bella grinned and joined in the dance.

So did dark-haired Sofia. And so did fun-loving Natalie.

"And we say HEY!

We're gonna dance the night away . . ." they sang together, twirling about in the centre of the room.

Veronica was dancing the salsa moves from Britney's video, so Bella, Natalie and Sofia copied her steps. *Left foot forward. Right rock back. Left foot back. Hold! Step back right. Rock forward left. Step forward right. Hold!*

Soon they were all whirling around, clapping and stamping, improvising a mad party salsa together.

Bella heard a laugh and turned to see Emma, their dorm monitor, standing in the doorway grinning. "Ay caramba!"

she cried and shimmied her way over.
"Now *THIS* is a proper way to start the
day!"

As the song finished, the five girls
cheered and applauded each other.
"That was *FUN*," Natalie beamed.

"Really cool," Sofia laughed. "The only thing is, all that shaking has messed up my hair!"

"Come down to breakfast when you're ready," said fifteen-year-old Emma. "I don't know about you guys, but I've worked up an appetite already."

"Me too," Bella said, feeling flushed and happy. Only at the Strictly Dance Academy could you have a salsa session before breakfast, she thought to herself with a smile. How lucky she was to be there!

As she had a last check in the mirror, her eye was caught by the photograph of her parents that she kept on her bedside table. It had been taken the summer before, when they'd holidayed in

Cornwall, and showed her mum and dad with tans and sunglasses smiling on the beach. Bella's mum had put it in a pretty purple frame and given it to her at the start of term. "Just so we're always with you," she'd said. "And so you know we'll always be thinking about you."

Bella had a sudden lump in her throat remembering how strange it had been to say goodbye to her parents back then, but in the next second she remembered something that cheered her up immediately. She was going to see them again tomorrow!

"Oh! Just one day until Parents' Day now!" she said to her friends. "I can't wait to see my mum and dad again."

"Me too," Sofia agreed. Tomorrow

was the academy's Parents' Day, where all the students' parents were invited to visit the school and see how their children were progressing. A special show had been rehearsed followed by a celebratory lunch for everyone. It was going to be wonderful! "I think my Nonna's coming too. Any excuse for a party," she added, fastening her hair into a plait with a grin. Sofia was Italian and came from a big, tight-knit family.

"My mom says she's about to explode, she's so excited," Natalie added. "So don't stand too near us, whatever you do."

Bella smiled. Natalie was American, but had been living in England for the past two years. She and her mum were very close, and spoke on the phone every day.

Veronica was the only one who remained quiet. "How about you, Veronica, are you looking forward to tomorrow?" Sofia asked.

Veronica was leaning into the mirror, applying lip gloss even though make-up was strictly forbidden until Year 10. "Sure," she said breezily. "Daddy said to give him a list of all the things I want for my birthday next month. He said he'd buy some early presents to keep me going."

Bella turned away. Veronica's family were obviously very rich because they seemed to send her new gifts and treats every week. It must be nice to

be showered with so much lovely stuff,
Bella had thought wistfully more than
once. Not only had Veronica been
sent her new MP3 player but just the
week before, the most gorgeous pair
of pale blue fluffy slippers had arrived
too, along with a brand new dressing
gown, wrapped in shiny silver paper
and tied with a huge pink ribbon. Bella
knew Veronica had her own pony back
home and a huge flat-screen TV in her
bedroom. She had spent Christmas in

the Bahamas, too, with
her parents and
her older brother.
"Mummy hates
the cold," Veronica
had said.

Bella, who'd spent Christmas with
her grandma and all her cousins, in a
noisy jumble of presents, chocolate and
excited dogs, couldn't imagine living
in such a glamorous world. Then she
glanced at the photo of her parents and
immediately felt disloyal for envying
Veronica.

"Let's go to breakfast," she said
quickly. "Come on!"

As ever, Bella's class spent the morning
having ordinary lessons – today it was
Maths, Science and History – before
the fun of dance classes could begin.
Bella always loved the moment that
the lunch bell rang to signal the end of
the morning. It was brilliant knowing

that the rest of the day would be spent dancing. Bliss!

As she and her friends went downstairs for lunch, Bella glanced out of the window in the stairwell and stopped dead as she saw a bright pink sports car cruising into the academy driveway. Whoa. Whose car was *that*?

"Wow," she breathed. "Look!"

Sofia nearly cannoned straight into her. "Bella!" she cried, just stopping in time. Then she too looked out of the window.

"Mamma mia!" she said. "That is the coolest car I've ever seen."

"Must belong to someone super-famous," Natalie commented, eyes wide. "Or super-rich. Hey, Veronica, I think your parents just arrived early!" she joked.

There was quite a cluster of people watching through the window now as the sports car drove sedately up the driveway and turned off into the staff car park. Veronica had to elbow her way through in order to see. "Don't be silly," she said, glimpsing the back of the pink car before it disappeared. "Mummy and Daddy have a Bentley. That kind of car is way too blingy for them."

"It wasn't too blingy for me," Bella

confessed as they set off down the stairs again. "I'd love a car like that, wouldn't you?"

"Too right," Natalie said. "Only I'd have a soft-top so that I could drive around with the top down, looking cool, with everyone seeing me."

"One day, when we're all famous dancers . . ." Sofia said dreamily as they joined the lunch queue.

"I wonder if it's one of the Strictly Come Dancing stars visiting?" Bella mused as she took a tray and cutlery. She and the other students were all massive fans of the show, and found it really exciting whenever they saw any of the professional dancers. The show was filmed very near the academy so the students sometimes caught glimpses of the dancers and judges arriving for rehearsals, or filming. "Wouldn't it be amazing if one of them was here to put on a masterclass for us?"

"You never know," Natalie said. "At the Strictly Dance Academy, anything is possible!"

**Read
Salsa Sparkle
to find out what
happens next!**

Meet the characters at the
Strictly Dance Academy

Character profile:

★ Favourite colour: blue

★ Favourite dance: the jive because Jason loves gelling his hair back retro style.

★ Favourite outfit: the blue leather jacket that Jason wore to Rock 'n' Roll!

★ Favourite accessory: Jason loves wearing hats and using them as props – like the trilby hat he wears in *Showdance Star*.

★ Favourite dance partner: Bella of course!

★ Jason started dancing when he was five years old.

Fun fact *Jason is the youngest of three – his older brother and sister are also dancers and they have won lots of competitions so he has lots to live up to!*

WIN AN IPOD SHUFFLE!

Read our Strictly Come Dancing books *Rock 'n' Rolling* and *Jumping Jive*, answer the questions below, and soon you could be practising your dance moves on the go with a fabulous iPod Shuffle!

QUESTION 1

What is the name of the West End musical Bella auditions for in *Rock 'n' Rolling*?

a) Grease
b) Slick
c) Hairspray

QUESTION 2

Which Hollywood star does Bella get to dance with in *Jumping Jive*?

a)   Jet Rogerson
b)   Jim Rocking
c)   Josh Robinson

JUST SEND YOUR ANSWERS, WITH YOUR NAME AND ADDRESS, ON A POSTCARD TO:

Strictly Come Dancing iPod Shuffle Competition, Marketing Department, Hodder Children's Books, 338 Euston Road, London, NW1 3BH.

BY 31 JANUARY 2013

Runner-up prizes are also available!

See full terms and conditions at www.hodderchildrens.co.uk

A STAGE ENTERTAINMENT AND PHIL MCINTYRE ENTERTAINMENT
IN ASSOCIATION WITH BBC WORLDWIDE PRESENTATION

THE LIVE TOUR

★ ★ ★ ★

'THE ULTIMATE
FEEL GOOD SHOW'

DAILY TELEGRAPH

THROUGHOUT THE UK
IN JAN AND FEB 2013
On sale autumn 2012

strictlycomedancinglive.com

Join our Review Crew and receive a free book!*

Be the first to read great new books!

The Review Crew are a group of passionate readers who help us by reviewing new and upcoming books before they've even hit the shops!

Members of the Review Crew receive free copies of our books in manuscript form and tell us what they think by filling in a simple questionnaire. We also like to ask for feedback about cover designs.

If you'd like to claim your free book and join the hundreds of other kids getting involved, just visit:

www.hachettechildrens.co.uk/reviewcrew

and sign up today!

Or, fill in the form overleaf and post to: Review Crew, Hachette Children's Books, 338 Euston Road, London, NW1 3BH

*All free books worth a minimum £3.99. Please allow 28 days for delivery. UK only.

First Name (in BLOCK capitals)..

Surname (in BLOCK capitals)..

Are you ☐ Male or ☐ Female?

Date of Birth: DAY ☐☐ MONTH ☐☐ YEAR ☐☐☐☐

Email Address..

Address...

....

....

Postcode..

If you are under 12 years old please ask a parent/guardian to sign below – otherwise we won't be able to send you anything!

Parent/Guardian Signature...

Name (in BLOCK capitals)..

Date...

As we can only send out a limited number of printed manuscripts, we would also like to be able to send you electronic versions of our books.

☐ Please tick this box if you either own or have access to an e-reader.